MW00887976

(Also found as far north as Nova Scotia and as far south as the Gulf of Mexico. Although the slipper shells are native to the Atlantic Ocean they have traveled on oysters and other shells to other countries and can now be found in Belgium, Denmark, France, Italy, the Netherlands, Spain, the U.K., Norway and Sweden.) footnotes: http://en.wikipedia.org/wiki/Common_slipper_shell

Text copyright © 2013 by Christi-Anne Haiduk
Illustrations by Lea Orsini

All rights reserved

ISBN-10: 1491253320
ISBN-13: 9781491253328
Library of Congress Control Number: 2013914065
Createspace Independent Publishing Platform
North Charleston, South Carolina

For my husband, John, with love.
Thank you for believing in me.

John, Noelle and Grace for always inspiring me.

Mom and Marci for all of your support. —CJH

For Mom, Dad and Ant —LO

Remember to look for Mermaid Slippers
at the Beach!
~ Be a Believer!!

Fins Forever,

C.J. Haiduk
-2016

This Book Belongs to:

MERMAID SLIPPERS

By C.J. Haiduk
Illustrated by Lea Orsini

Most people don't know the truth about mermaids.

Most people don't look for the signs.

What most people need to know about mermaids is that they are very tiny in size.

We all tend to think that they are the size of humans and therefore miss seeing them in our everyday lives...

Yet, they are with us, every day, especially in the summer, which is their favorite time of year. This is the magical time when humans come to the beaches and the mermaids come out to play.

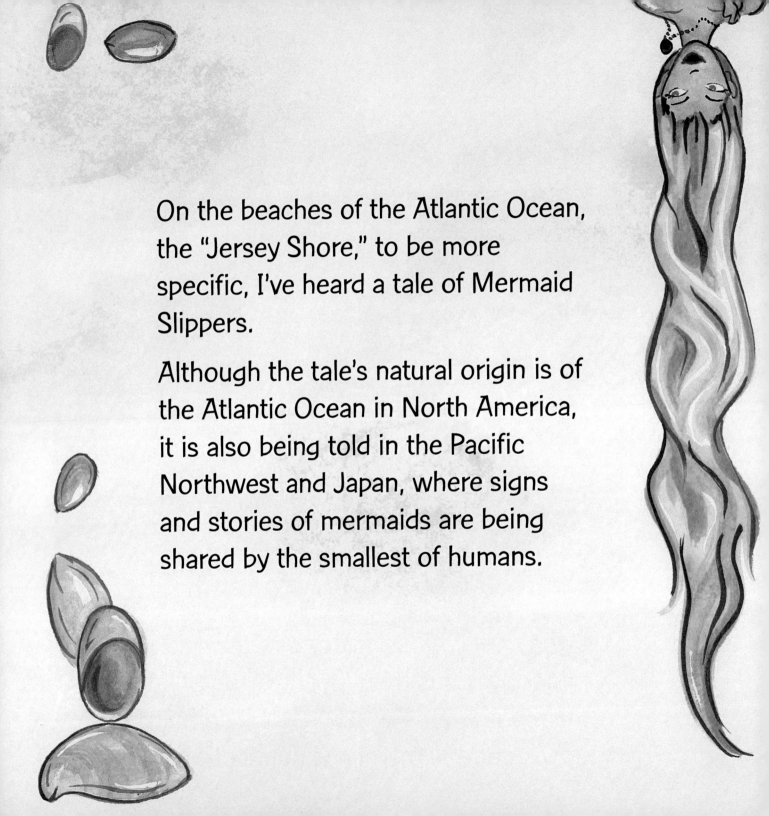

On the beaches of the Atlantic Ocean, the "Jersey Shore," to be more specific, I've heard a tale of Mermaid Slippers.

Although the tale's natural origin is of the Atlantic Ocean in North America, it is also being told in the Pacific Northwest and Japan, where signs and stories of mermaids are being shared by the smallest of humans.

ASIA

NORTH AMERICA

the
PACIFIC

N
W E
S

Children from all
over the world are
the witnesses of this
mystic tale.

Parents from many countries such as Belgium, Denmark, France, and Italy are so very proud of their children's "colorful imaginations" as the tale is spreading.

Stories of mermaids are continuously being reported in the Netherlands, Spain, and the U.K. The latest news has recently come in from Norway and Sweden where the Mermaid Slippers are now appearing in abundance.

These slippers are the only evidence that mermaids do exist. Most children have many experiences to share and at least one slipper in their shell collection.

Listen closely, the tale goes like this;

Each and every morning, when the sun rises, the mermaids swim up to the surface of the ocean.

The waves carry them onto the sandy beaches. Their bodies dry off in the sun and their feet appear. Now they are ready to explore.

This is when they search for their Mermaid Slippers. You may have seen them, in your travels. Non-believers call them slipper shells. Believers call them, Mermaid Slippers.

Mermaid Slippers are little shells that are oftentimes white or light in color. They can be polka dotted or striped, but they are always half moon shaped with a little covering inside for a mermaid's tiny foot to fit into.

Sometimes the mermaids put on the wrong size and clumsily fall around. That is part of the fun, but eventually they always find the right pair of slippers that fit perfectly, and this is when their adventures begin.

When they are all in their slippers, the mermaids come together. They hold hands and sing their "Glory to the Day" song. The song is the same in any land, as the mermaids have their own universal language.

To us it would sound like a peaceful wind or an ocean breeze that fills our hearts with joy.

The meaning of the words when translated into English are:

Thankful for each blessed day of happiness and joy, the feeling of togetherness with human girls and boys, sharing sun, the beach and sea, where all of life begins,

—Oh how wonderful to share the days without our fins.

Soon after, the humans arrive at the beach, dragging chairs, umbrellas, coolers and towels.

This is like a playground for the mermaids, who find humans to be fascinating creatures.

For some reason human adults are so busy in their thoughts that they just don't see the mermaids, who are very silly and playful beings.

The mermaids absolutely adore playing with human babies and small children.

You see, since babies can't talk, the mermaids can interact very closely with them.

They love to make them laugh.

The mermaids spread themselves out along the beach so they are not easily seen.

A bell can be heard every hour in the afternoon. It's the ice cream man! He stands near the dunes ringing his bell to invite all of the families to come and enjoy some delicious and refreshing cold treats.

The mermaids find creative ways to get a taste.

Young children sometimes very innocently tell their parents about the mermaids but no one believes them.

"Look, Mommy, the pretty mermaid braided my hair."

— "That's nice, honey".

"See our beautiful sand castle, Daddy! We decorated the sides with mermaid hair."

— "Very clever."

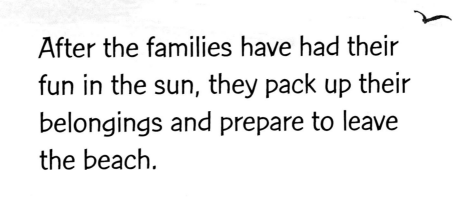

After the families have had their fun in the sun, they pack up their belongings and prepare to leave the beach.

Although, like human children, mermaids can be spunky, they do try to be kind and polite.

They always wave goodbye to the children they were lucky enough to spend the day with.

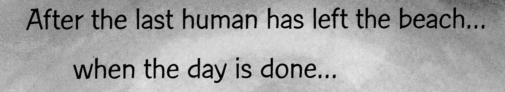

After the last human has left the beach...

when the day is done...

before the sun fully sets...

the mermaids feast on sand crabs with jellyfish and seaweed salad.

When the feast has ended, again they gather with happy hearts for the day they have shared with humans.

All of the mermaids scatter their slippers on the beach, in mixed pairs, so that no one can tell they were there.

They return home to the sea, looking forward to tomorrow's adventures.

Do you have a Mermaid Slipper in your shell collection?

Are you a believer?

25780254R00022

Made in the USA
San Bernardino, CA
11 November 2015